Published by Orange Hat Publishing 2020
ISBN 978-1-64538-174-7

Copyright © 2020 by Elliott Lee
All Rights Reserved
Jupiter the Alpha Planet
Written by Elliott Lee
Illustrated by Philip Hurst

For information, please contact:

Orange Hat Publishing
www.orangehatpublishing.com
Waukesha, WI

JUPITER
the Alpha Planet

Written by **Elliott Lee**

Illustrated by **Philip Hurst**

Once upon a space time continuum,
the meanest meteor in the Milky Way
crashed into the Sun.

The Sun got knocked out of its orbit.

Loosed from galactic shackles,
the searing Sun drifted closer
to Mercury, Venus, Earth, and Mars.

The four planets were at risk
of being burned to a crisp.

They became extremely scared.
They couldn't get out from their orbit.

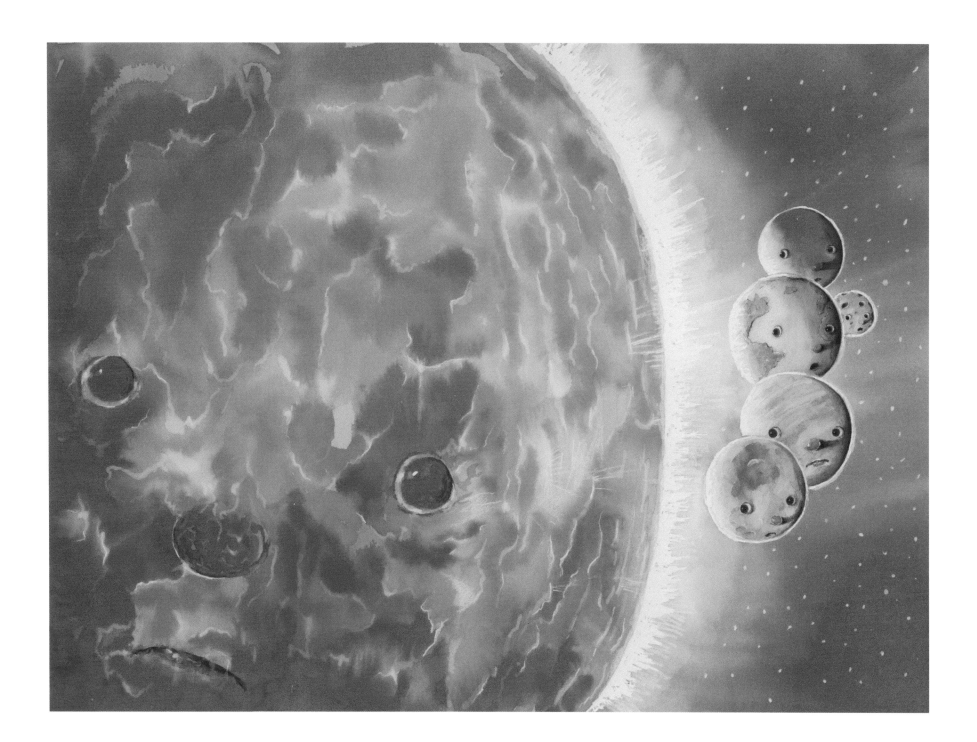

"Help us outer planets!" they shouted.

Luckily, though millions of miles away,
Jupiter heard them.

It quickly made a shelter for them
in its enormous storm spot.

One by one,
Mercury, Venus, Earth, and Mars
huddled in the storm spot.

They were safe!

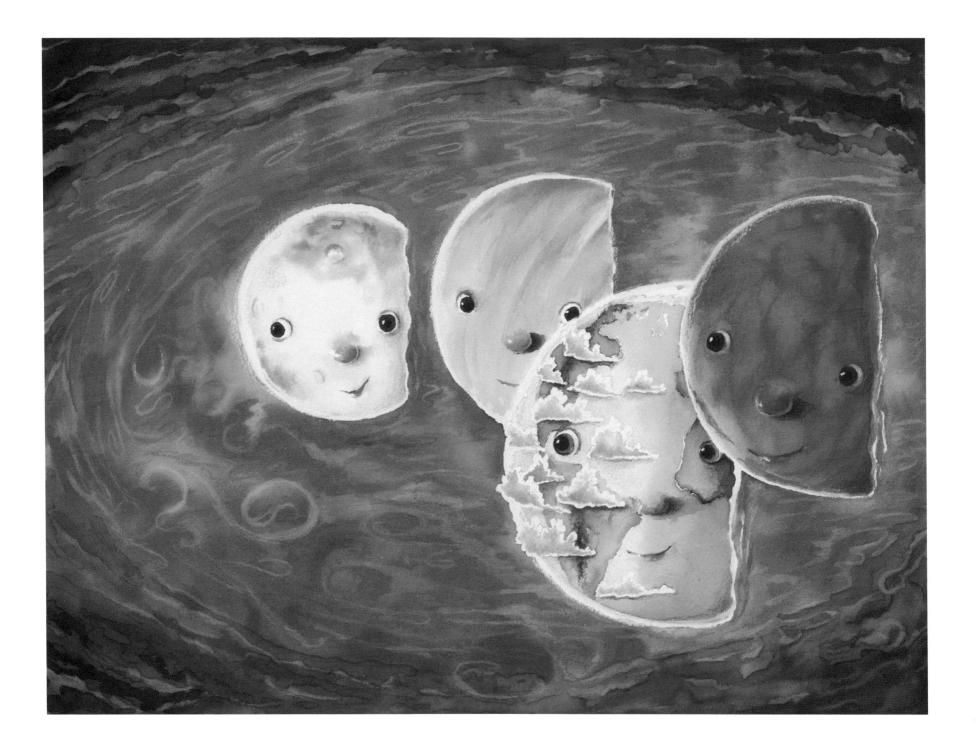

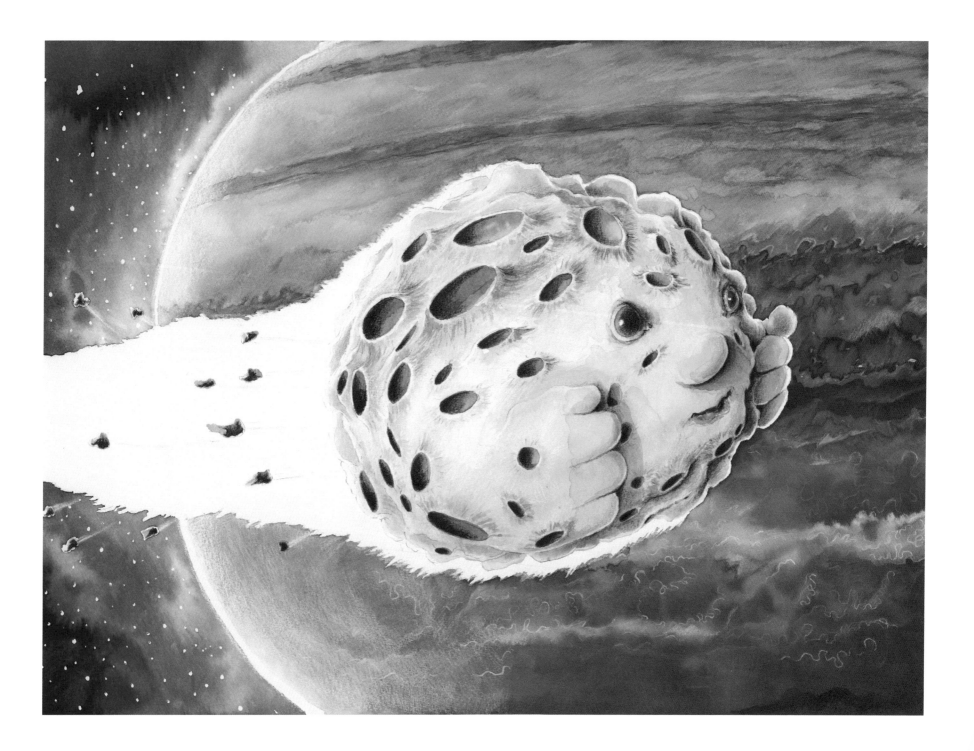

Suddenly, the mean meteor
went after Jupiter, blasting toward
the gas giant's core.

However, being so massive,
Jupiter was not worried.

The force of its gravity
quickly broke the mean meteor
into tiny space rocks and dust.

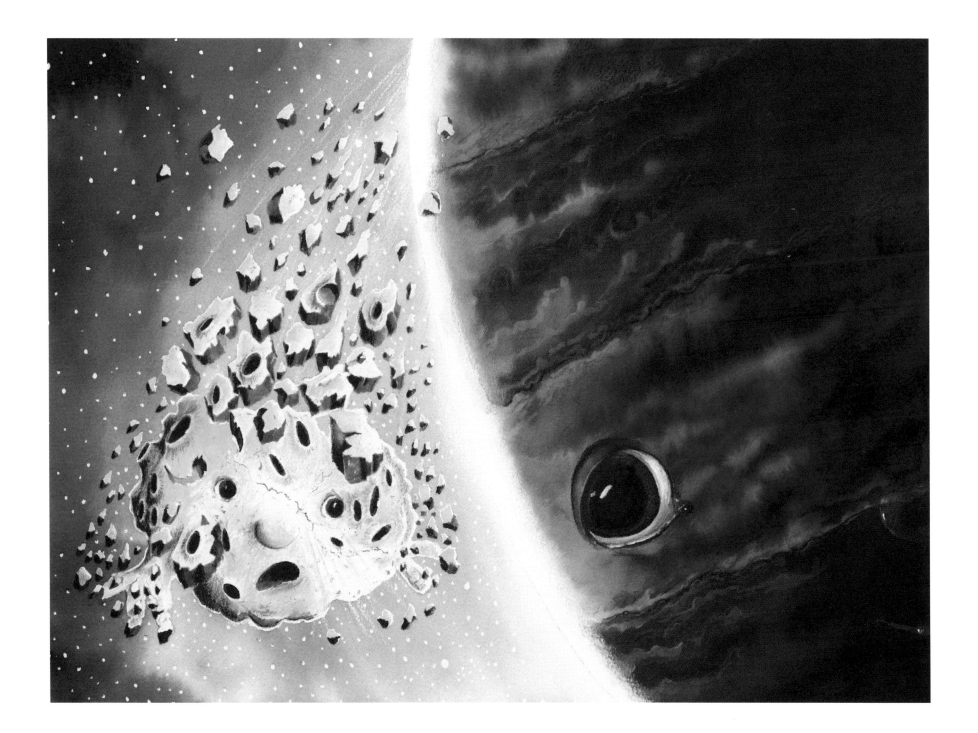

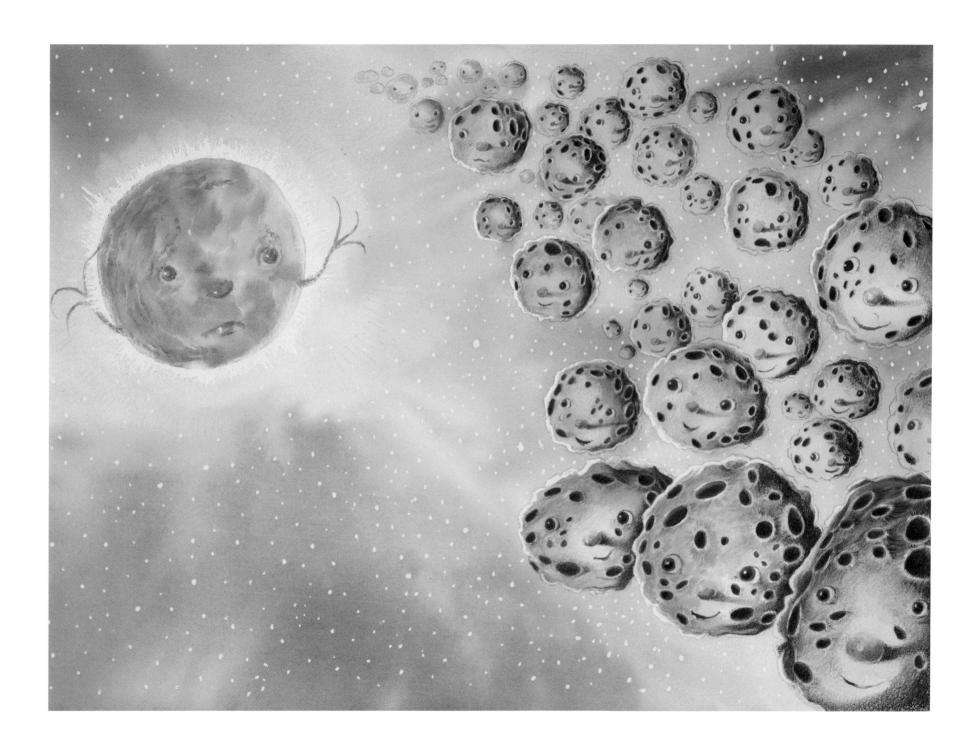

As the Sun continued to soar
out of the solar system,
it asked all the asteroids, comets,
and small ice bodies for help.

They quickly joined together
and the entire Kuiper Belt was assembled.

The Kuiper Belt was slightly larger
than the Sun, and like a baseball bat,
it knocked the Sun back
into the solar system.

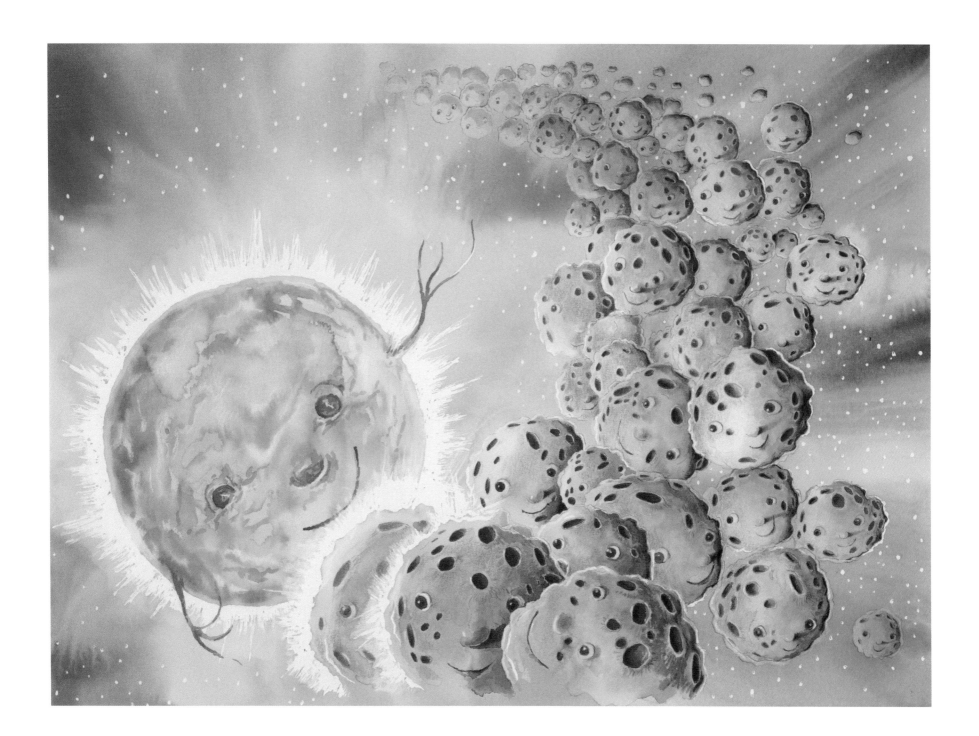

The planets were saved.
Mercury, Venus, Earth, and Mars
were back in their orbit.

They all cheered.
"Thank you, Jupiter, for saving us!
Thank you, Kuiper Belt!"

The Sun also was very happy
and relieved that it was back
in its original place.

The mean meteor was gone.

All continued on their rounds
circling in the infinite sea of space.

CPSIA information can be obtained at www.ICGtesting.com
Printed in the USA
BVIW120906101120
592384BV00003B/2